Deleted

Deleted

Montezuma's Revenge

by Cari Best

pictures by Diane Palmisciano

ORCHARD BOOKS   NEW YORK

For Honey—who finally
got hers
　　　　　—C.B.

For Catharine, Clio, and Daisy
　　　　　—D.P.

Orchard Books, A Grolier Company
95 Madison Avenue, New York, NY 10016

Manufactured in the United States of America
Printed and bound by Phoenix Color Corp.
The text of this book is set in 15 point Minion and 14.5 Gill Sans Regular.
The illustrations are oil pastel.
10 9 8 7 6 5 4 3 2 1

Library of Congress Cataloging-in-Publication Data
Best, Cari. Montezuma's Revenge / by Cari Best ; illustrated by
Diane Palmisciano.
p. cm. Summary: Left behind when his family goes to the beach, Montezuma
the dog gets revenge by bringing home a scruffy dog he meets in the park and
giving him the run of the house.
ISBN 0-531-30198-2 (trade : alk. paper).—ISBN 0-531-33198-9 (lib. : alk. paper)
[1. Dogs—Fiction.] I. Palmisciano, Diane, ill.
PZ7.B46575Mo 1999 [E]—dc21 99-11716

The minute Montezuma smelled the suitcases,

he knew that Sally and Steve
and his best buddy, Sam,
were going away.
Again.

Sit! he barked. **Stay!** he barked.
But Sally and Steve and his best buddy, Sam, kept right on packing.
Swimsuits and sandals, shorts and shirts. Buckets and shovels and bunches of books.
Oh boy—the beach! barked Montezuma, getting his ball.

I'm a good dog! he barked, wagging hopefully. You always say I am. But Sally and Steve and his best buddy, Sam, kept right on going. Out of the bedroom and through the hall. Down the stairs and out the door.

"See you later, Monty," said Sally.
Like she always did.

"*Bone* voyage," said Steve.
Like he always did.

"I wish you could *come*," said Sam.
Like he always did.

But the minute Montezuma made his move,
Sally said, "Sit!"
And Steve said, "Stay!"
Sam said, "Good dog!"
And they all went away.
Just like they always did.

How come I'm the only one who ever listens? thought Montezuma, preparing himself to sit and to stay. Just like he always did.

There's nothing worse than being left behind, Montezuma moaned, listening to the clock tick and the faucet drip. Unless you're left behind with Darryl—the detestable dog-sitter. I'll bet Darryl's on his way over right now. Montezuma's stomach sank as he remembered Darryl's smell. Damp—like a wet mop.

Here you are, girl.

Mont

He gives me my dinner without any cheese, Montezuma complained.

And he rubs me the wrong way—so that all my fur sticks up like a really bad haircut.

Darryl thinks all dogs are girls. And he doesn't even know my name.

Oh misery!

Montezuma missed his family more than ever.

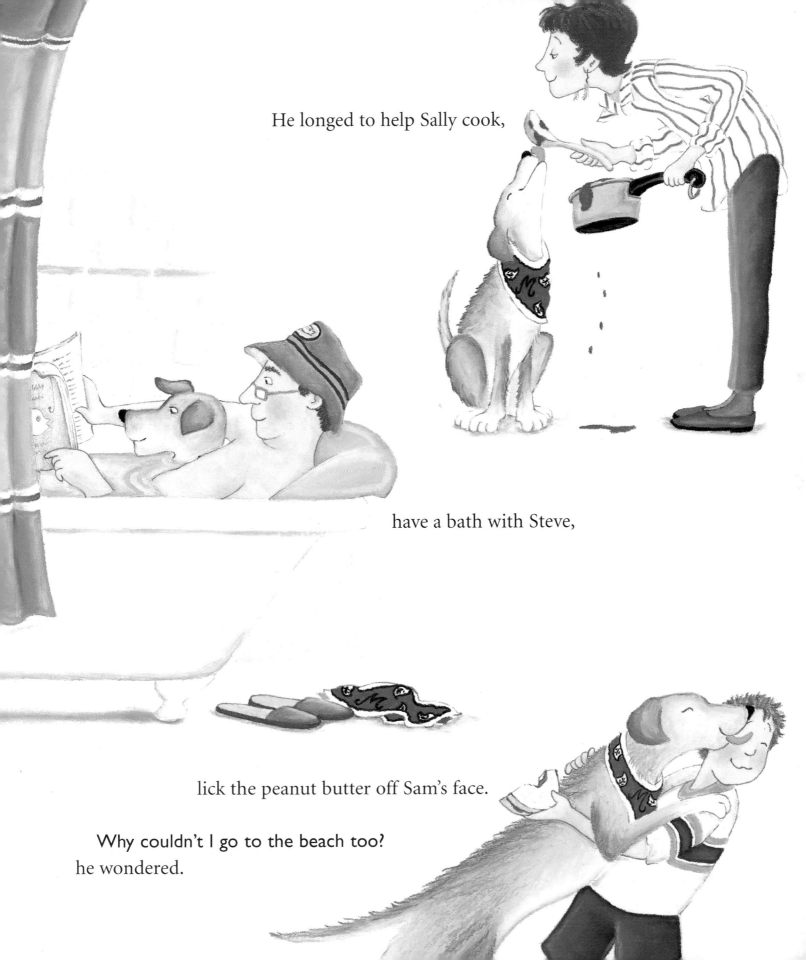

He longed to help Sally cook,

have a bath with Steve,

lick the peanut butter off Sam's face.

Why couldn't I go to the beach too?
he wondered.

The more Montezuma
thought about being left behind,
the hotter under the collar he got.

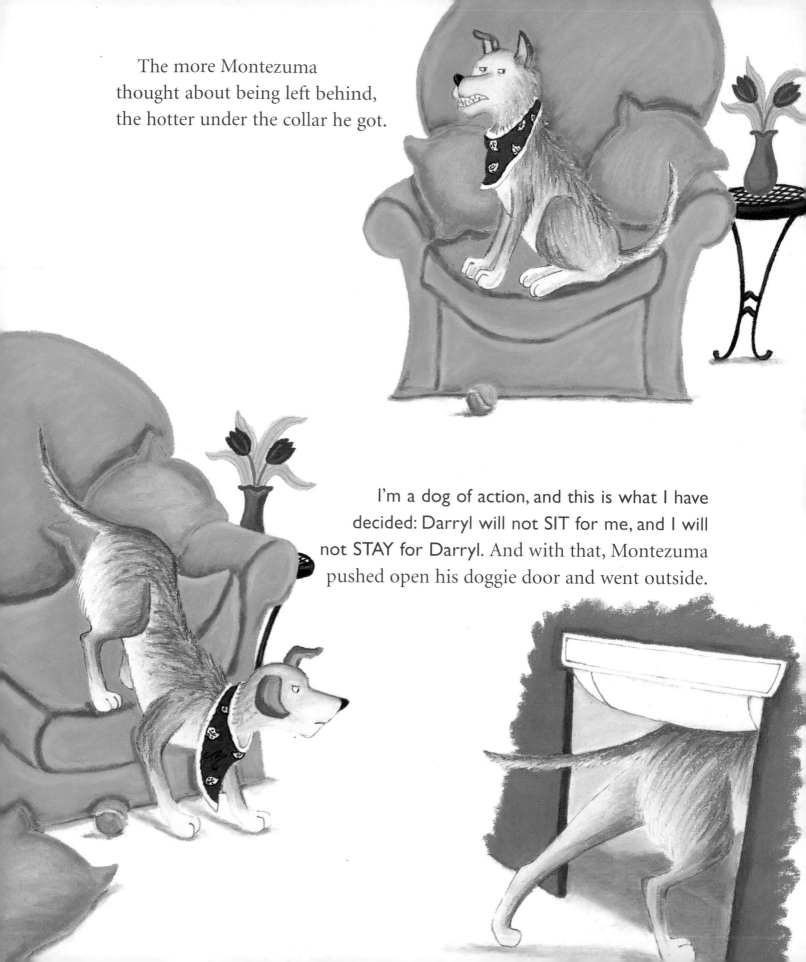

I'm a dog of action, and this is what I have
decided: Darryl will not SIT for me, and I will
not STAY for Darryl. And with that, Montezuma
pushed open his doggie door and went outside.

I have to do something to get my family to pay attention when I bark. But what? he asked himself. I could go on vacation too.

Couldn't I?

But good dog that he was, Montezuma felt that he had to keep a watchful eye on his house.

No matter what.

To take his mind off his troubles, Montezuma had himself a pleasant stroll around the block, stopping at all the usual places. He skipped off to the park, where he had a good romp,

ate somebody's leftover lunch,
        and took a refreshing drink from the fountain.

Then, feeling tired, he flopped down and had a snooze in a shady space under a bench.

After some time, he was sharply awakened by a strange bark.

My name's Wild Bill, and I own that shade.

There before him stood the scruffiest dog he had ever seen—
or smelled. The dog drooled and the dog spit.
He itched and he twitched. He was musty
and he was moldy.

Montezuma was mesmerized. My name's Monty, he barked back. And I have a family, but they're at the beach. Montezuma's heart thumped, and he felt weak in the knees.

The beach is okay, but I've been to the Okefenokee Swamp, answered Wild Bill, who had been around the block a few times himself. And I never visit the same place twice.

Then he told Montezuma about all the other places he'd gone, and Montezuma told him all about his house and his family.

Is there any place you haven't been? barked Montezuma respectfully.

Wild Bill thought awhile: Well, I've always wanted to see the inside of one of those houses. He pointed with his nose. Like the one you live in.

Then it was Montezuma's turn to think awhile. Hey, Wild Bill, he
finally barked. How'd you like to be my family's dog-for-a-day?

They talked it over and came up with a plan. Montezuma couldn't
wait for his family to come home.

And come home they did, one week later.
"I have kisses for Monty!" sang Sally.
"Go fetch your ball, Monty baby!" shouted Steve.
"Come and get your treats, Monty!" called Sam.

But for the first time ever,
Montezuma didn't come when he was called.

Sally looked high and Steve looked low,
and Sam looked everywhere in between.
There was no Montezuma by the front door.

And no Montezuma in the den.

No Montezuma in the closet,

and none in the doghouse either.

"Wherever could he be?" asked Sally.
"I wish I knew," said Steve.
"Here, good dog," coaxed Sam,
trying the peanut butter trick.
But Montezuma didn't come—not
even for that.

That's when they heard the noise. It was a strange noise, like laughing and scratching and howling and yowling all rolled into one. The family rushed into the bedroom and held their breath— and their noses.

There was Wild Bill having the time of his life—
jumping up and down on the bed,
splashing in the toilet, and
swinging on the drapes.

Pleased to meet you all, he barked. I'm your
dog-for-a-day while my good friend Monty
attends to some important business.

Sally was stunned.
Steve got the shivers.
Sam sneezed.
But Wild Bill didn't seem
to notice.

He was too busy sampling Sally's lipsticks, trying on Steve's pajamas, riding Sam's skateboard, and eating Montezuma's family out of house and home.

"Sit!" screamed Sally.

"Stay!" ordered Steve.

"Come!" yelled Sam. But Wild Bill kept right on going. Out of the bedroom and through the hall. Down the stairs and out the door. I don't do SITS and I don't do STAYS. I don't do COMES either, he barked. And Wild Bill, who never visited the same place twice, was off to the next.

A short time later, Sally and Steve and Sam were still looking for Montezuma.

"Monty was the best dog," Sally said. "He always listened."

"And he never smelled," said Steve. "Or scratched."

"I knew we should have taken him to the beach with us," said Sam. "And on all our other vacations too. I'd do anything to hold him now."

That's all Montezuma needed to hear. He bounded out from behind the bushes (where he had been guarding his house all along) and showered his family with I-missed-you kisses and I-love-you licks. **Wasn't my friend Wild Bill something else?** he barked.

"Oh, Monty, we're so glad you're home," his family said, this time listening to his every bark.

Good Dog

Now, the minute Montezuma smells the suitcases, he knows that Sally and Steve and his best buddy, Sam, are going away. But he never has to worry. Not ever again. Because Sally and Steve and his best buddy, Sam, always ask him to come along.